11·19 **DATE DUE**

DEC 0 7 2019	
DEC 2 6 2019	
5·28·21	

For my daughters, Elana and Sonia, whose lives continue to inspire me
—S. E. R.

For Grams, where my love of birds began
—S. F. C.

Acknowledgments
The author wishes to thank Al Sgroi, for his intrepid leadership on the
Christmas Bird Count, and Andy Magee, who organizes the Concord Area Count
Circle for my Acton territory. Thanks also to my editor, Vicky Holifield, who believed
in this book; Pamela Sowizral, birding partner extraordinaire, who reviewed the bird
descriptions; my Concord SCBWI group, who kept me writing and rewriting;
my parents, James and Nancy Edwards; and my husband, Jim, for whose love
and support I am eternally grateful.

Published by
Peachtree Publishing Company Inc.
1700 Chattahoochee Avenue
Atlanta, Georgia 30318-2112
www.peachtree-online.com

Text © 2019 by Susan Edwards Richmond
Illustrations © 2019 by Stephanie Fizer Coleman

Edited by Vicky Holifield
Design and composition by Nicola Simmonds Carmack
The illustrations were rendered digitally.

Printed in January 2019 by Tien Wah Press, Malaysia
10 9 8 7 6 5 4 3 2 1
First Edition
ISBN 978-1-56145-954-4

Library of Congress Cataloging-in-Publication Data

Names: Richmond, Susan Edwards, author. | Coleman, Stephanie Fizer, illustrator.
Title: Bird count / written by Susan Edwards Richmond; illustrated by Stephanie Fizer Coleman.
Description: Atlanta : Peachtree Publishing Company Inc., [2018] | Summary: An excited young girl and her mother carefully participate in the
Christmas Bird Count as part of a team of citizen scientists, tallying birds found in different habitats near their home. Includes facts about birding
and why the Christmas Bird Count is important.
Identifiers: LCCN 2018036825 | ISBN 9781561459544
Subjects: | CYAC: Birds—Fiction. | Scientists—Fiction. | Counting.
Classification: LCC PZ7.1.R5337 Bir 2018 | DDC [E]—dc23
LC record available at *https://lccn.loc.gov/2018036825*

BIRD COUNT

Susan Edwards Richmond

Illustrated by Stephanie Fizer Coleman

PEACHTREE
ATLANTA

I shake Mom in the dark. "Wake up, sleepy head! It's Bird Count Day."

One Sunday each winter we take part in a bird census called the Christmas Bird Count. On this day, we go out and count every bird we see or hear.

Mom says helping with the bird count makes us citizen scientists. Citizen scientists are ordinary people who do real science research. We aren't the only ones, either. Today, from the far north of Canada all the way down to Antarctica, people are counting birds.

"Bundle up, Ava," Mom says. "It's cold outside."

I find my fuzzy hat and my warmest coat. I'm glad we're not birding in Antarctica!

Knock! Knock!

It's Big Al. He's our team leader. There are ten teams in our count circle. Each team counts the birds in one area.

Our team follows the same route every year—fields, woods, wetlands, neighborhoods. Even the center of town!

You never know where you'll find birds.

"Hey, Ava," says Big Al. "What are the rules again?"

He knows I know them, but he tests me every time.

"Count every bird you see or hear," I tell him. "Make sure at least two people see or hear it. And don't count any bird twice."

The last one is hard, but we do our best.

"Did you bring the scientist's most important tools?" asks Big Al.

Mom's got our binoculars, I've got the field guide, and Big Al has a notebook and pencil. But that's not what he means.

"Our eyes and ears," I say.

"That's right," says Big Al.

It's still dark when we back out of our driveway.

I roll down my window and hear an owl.

Who's awake? Me tooo, it calls.

We can't see it, but we all hear it. So it counts.

"Why don't you take the tally today, Ava?"
Big Al hands me the notebook.

I look at Mom and smile. This is my first time.

I write **great horned owl** at the top of the page
and make a single mark.

Chick-a-dee-dee-dee, a **chickadee** calls good morning. I add it to the list. I'm going to be busy today!

GREAT HORNED OWL - 1
CHICKADEE - 1

As the sun comes up, a V of birds flies overhead. Long necks, slow wingbeats.

"**Canada geese** flying over!" I make four up-and-down slash marks and one across for a bundle of five.

"That's the way to tally," says Big Al.

I'm keeping an eye out for a big black bird called a raven. I saw one two years ago, but not last year. Big Al says ravens are rare around here. I hope we'll see mine again today!

GREAT HORNED OWL - 1
CHICKADEE - 1
CANADA GOOSE - ℍℱ

"Let's check out this field," says Big Al, shooing us from the truck.

It's freezing, but birds don't mind. Eight small birds dip and glide, dip and glide, right at us, then veer away.

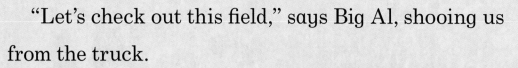

Goldfinches aren't gold in winter, so the color won't help us. But we know them by the way they fly.

One bundle of five and three straight marks.

A bigger bird jumps to the top of a bush. I lose sight of it for a moment. Then it flaps away in a flash of gray and white. Mockingbird markings!

But Mom and Al missed it. So it doesn't count.

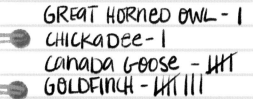

GREAT HORNED OWL - I
CHICKADEE - I
CANADA GOOSE - ᄔᄔᄔ
GOLDFINCH - ᄔᄔᄔ III

"Nothing flying right now," Big Al observes. We scan the trees, looking for familiar shapes.

"Tallest oak," Mom whispers. "Two o'clock."

Big Al and I read the tree like a big clock face, with noon at the top and six at the bottom.

There it is, a big bird of prey with its feathers fluffed up. Its back is brown, its belly white.

One **red-tailed hawk.**

"Let's find its mate," Al says. He and Mom search the other trees. But I stick with the same tree, sure the other hawk is there.

I check the tree again. "Six o'clock," I say. "Close to the trunk."

"Good eye, Ava," says Big Al.

GREAT HORNED OWL - 1
CHICKADEE - 1
CANADA GOOSE - LHT
GOLDFINCH - LHT III
RED-TAILED HAWK - II

As we drive to our next stop, I watch the sky out the window. A black bird soars above us. Its wings tilt up in a wide, flat V. It can't be my raven. That's the way a vulture flies. I look hard and see two more, higher up and making wobbly circles.

"Cool," Mom says.

Turkey vultures. Three hatch marks.

GREAT HORNED OWL - 1
CHICKADEE - 1
CANADA GOOSE - ⟍⟋⟍⟋⟍
GOLDFINCH - ⟍⟋⟍⟋⟍ III
RED-TAILED HAWK - II
TURKEY VULTURE - III

At Weatherbee Street, we park and walk down to the marsh. Loud quacks come from the cattails.

When we get closer, we see some ducks dipping their heads under the water, looking for food. *Splash!* Three other ducks dive out of sight. The "dabblers" are **mallards**, bottoms sticking up. The "divers" are **mergansers**. I tally them in our notebook.

Everything's quiet for a while, then we spot a quiver in the tall reeds. A hungry **great blue heron** stretches its long neck, on the lookout for a tasty fish.

My stomach growls. Scientists get hungry, too!

GREAT HORNED OWL - 1
CHICKADEE - 1
CANADA GOOSE - IIII
GOLDFINCH - IIIIIIII
RED-TAILED HAWK - II
TURKEY VULTURE - III
MALLARD - III
MERGANSER - IIII
GREAT BLUE HERON - I

As we head to lunch, we see a line of cars stopped ahead. Big Al stamps on the brake. I crane my head out the window to look. A flock of wild turkeys blocks the street between Crosby's Gas and Bagel Bin.

GREAT HORNED OWL - 1
CHICKADEE - 1
CANADA GOOSE - ⧠⧠⧠⧠⧠
GOLDFINCH - ⧠⧠⧠⧠⧠ III
RED-TAILED HAWK - II
TURKEY VULTURE - III
MALLARD - III
MERGANSER - IIII
GREAT BLUE HERON - 1
WILD TURKEY ⑰
STARLING - ⑫

We count. It's a big number, so I write 17 on the tally page and circle it.

While we wait for the traffic to start moving again, we count **starlings** in the trees. I count 11. Mom gets 12, but Al counts 13. I take the average of the three and circle the number 12.

Stomachs full, we drive through several neighborhoods. We're looking for feeders where birds gather.

"Stop," I say. "There's one with **cardinals,
blue jays, juncos.** Wait—and isn't that a
brown creeper on that tree? Its feathers look
just like the bark!"

"You're getting good at this," says Big Al.

I see a squirrel and a chipmunk, too. But
they don't count.

GREAT HORNED OWL - I
CHICKADEE - I
CANADA GOOSE - IIII
GOLDFINCH - IIII III
RED-TAILED HAWK - II
TURKEY VULTURE - III
MALLARD - III
MERGANSER - IIII
GREAT BLUE HERON - I
WILD TURKEY (17)
STARLING - (12)
CARDINAL - III
BLUE JAY - II
JUNCO - II
BROWN CREEPER - I

Whoosh! A hawk with a striped tail dives at the feeder. The small birds scatter. They came to eat seeds, but the larger bird came to eat them!

That's one **Cooper's hawk** for us.

GREAT HORNED OWL – 1
CHICKADEE – 1
CANADA GOOSE – ⅢⅠ
GOLDFINCH – ⅢⅠⅢ
RED-TAILED HAWK – ⅠⅠ
TURKEY VULTURE – ⅠⅠⅠ
MALLARD – ⅠⅠⅠ
MERGANSER – ⅠⅠⅠⅠ
GREAT BLUE HERON – 1
WILD TURKEY ⑰
STARLING – ⑫
CARDINAL – ⅠⅠⅠ
BLUE JAY – ⅠⅠ
JUNCO – ⅠⅠ
BROWN CREEPER – 1
COOPER'S HAWK – 1
CROW – 1

A big black bird wasn't scared away. It hops across the yard.

Is that my raven?

Caw caw. A **crow**, not a raven. Ravens make a croaking sound. I point it out to Mom and Big Al. Every bird counts!

On Horseshoe Lane, houses hide deep in
the woods. Someone reported seeing an ovenbird
here last week. Big Al says that ovenbirds
usually fly south to Central America before
now. As scientists, we need to investigate.

We make "pishing" sounds to bring out the ovenbird.

Pssshh, pssshh, pssshh.

We don't see an ovenbird, but we do hear a **downy woodpecker**'s *rat tat tat* on a trunk. Several little chickadees cock their heads at us. (We're miles from our last **chickadee**, so these go on the list, too.)

Pssshh, pssshh. Still no ovenbird.

We hear a sound like a cat's meow.

Then we see it, a gray bird with a flicking tail. It's a **catbird**!

GREAT HORNED OWL – I
CHICKADEE – HH I
CANADA GOOSE – HH
GOLDFINCH – HH III
RED-TAILED HAWK – II
TURKEY VULTURE – III
MALLARD – III
MERGANSER – IIII
GREAT BLUE HERON – I
WILD TURKEY (17)
STARLING – (12)
CARDINAL – III
BLUE JAY – II
JUNCO – II
BROWN CREEPER – I
COOPER'S HAWK – I
CROW – I
DOWNY WOODPECKER – I
CATBIRD – I

Back on the road, I see movement in Cucurbit Farm's fields. "Geese in the cornstalks!"

"Count 'em," says Big Al.

"One, two, three, four, five."

"Uh-oh," says Mom. "That's the same number as our flying flock. They probably landed here."

No hatch marks this time. We already tallied these geese.

GREAT HORNED OWL - 1
CHICKADEE - ‖‖ ‖
CANADA GOOSE - ‖‖
GOLDFINCH - ‖‖ ‖‖
RED-TAILED HAWK - ‖
TURKEY VULTURE - ‖‖
MALLARD - ‖‖
MERGANSER - ‖‖‖
GREAT BLUE HERON - 1
WILD TURKEY (17)
STARLING - (12)
CARDINAL - ‖‖
BLUE JAY - ‖
JUNCO - ‖
BROWN CREEPER - 1
COOPER'S HAWK - 1
CROW - 1
DOWNY WOODPECKER - 1
CATBIRD - 1
MOCKINGBIRD - 1

Big Al points to a gray-and-white bird.
"Look, Ava," he says. "There's your
mockingbird!" This time it counts.

As the sun sets, we pull into my school parking lot.
Behind rows of buses are trees full of birds. They're like
cutout shapes against the sky, but we can hear them.

Cedar waxwings *chittering.* **Mourning doves**
coo-hooing. **Robins** singing *cheerio, cheerio, cheerio.*

I see a big black bird flap to the ground. Looks like a
crow, but—

Groawk, groawk! it cries.

"That's it!" I shout. "My **raven** came back!"

GREAT HORNED OWL - 1
CHICKADEE - IIII I
CANADA GOOSE - IIII
GOLDFINCH - IIII III
RED-TAILED HAWK - II
TURKEY VULTURE - III
MALLARD - III
MERGANSER - IIII
GREAT BLUE HERON - 1
WILD TURKEY (17)
STARLING - (12)
CARDINAL - III
BLUE JAY - II
JUNCO - II
BROWN CREEPER - 1
COOPER'S HAWK - 1
CROW - 1
DOWNY WOODPECKER - 1
CATBIRD - 1
MOCKINGBIRD - 1
CEDAR WAXWING - III
MOURNING DOVE - II
ROBIN - IIII
RAVEN - 1

Too dark now to bird. But not too dark for a party!
Potluck, hot chocolate, firelight.

We meet other teams in our count circle, and share
what we saw. Big Al gives our tally to the circle chief.
She reports for all ten teams.

I love being a citizen scientist. Maybe someday I *will*
go to Antarctica on a bird count. I wonder what birds
I'd find there?

GREAT HORNED OWL - 1
CHICKADEE - IIII I
Canada Goose - IIII
GOLDFINCH - IIII IIII
RED-TAILED HAWK - II
TURKEY VULTURE - III
MALLARD - III
MERGANSER - IIII
GREAT BLUE HERON - 1
WILD TURKEY (17)
STARLING - (12)
CARDINAL - III
BLUE JAY - II
JUNCO - II
BROWN CREEPER - 1
COOPER'S HAWK - 1
CROW - 1
DOWNY WOODPECKER - 1
CATBIRD - 1
MOCKINGBIRD - 1
CEDAR WAXWING - III
MOURNING DOVE - II
ROBIN - IIII
Raven - 1

Blue jay: Although it has its own distinct calls, a jay can mimic a hawk. Acorns are a favorite food, so the blue jay may help in the spread of oak forests.

Brown creeper: This tiny bird with a long, down-curved bill spirals up huge trees searching for insects on the trunks and under bark.

Canada goose: Historically a fall migrant, many Canada geese now remain north all year and can be seen flying in their V formations between fields and open water.

Cardinal (Northern): Few sights are more welcome than the red blaze of a male cardinal against the winter snow. Cardinals are attracted to feeders filled with sunflower seeds.

Catbird (gray): The catbird's mewing cry is unmistakable. This slate-colored bird has a dark cap and rust-colored feathers under the tail.

Cedar waxwing: With its crest and upright posture, black mask, and sleek gray feathers, this bird always appears dressed for a formal occasion.

Chickadee (black-capped): A common visitor at backyard bird feeders, chickadees often flock with nuthatches, downy woodpeckers, and other species in winter.

Cooper's hawk: This hawk's swift, shadowy form is a common sight near backyard bird feeders, where it may snatch smaller birds that come for the seeds.

Crow (American): In winter you may see large flocks of several hundred crows or more. Crows have been known to make and use tools out of sticks and pine cones.

Downy woodpecker: This small bird can forage in places that larger woodpeckers have trouble reaching, such as small branches and weed stems.

Goldfinch (American): During the winter months, the male trades its brilliant yellow plumage for olive green. Goldfinches glean seeds from thistle and milkweed stalks.

Great blue heron: This heron flies with slow, stately wingbeats and with its long neck curved in a delicate S. Despite being 3 to 4 feet (approximately 1 meter) tall, these herons weigh only 5 to 6 pounds (2 to 3 kilograms)!

Great horned owl: Named for the two feathery tufts on its head, this fierce predator lives in woodlands, deserts, and wetlands, where it hunts mice and other small animals at night.

Junco (dark-eyed): This bird appears in the middle latitudes each winter and migrates farther north come spring. The junco flashes white outer tail feathers as it flies.

Mallard: The male is easily identified by its rounded bright green head. The female's drabber garb provides camouflage for when she is on her nest or with her young.

Merganser (common): The male sports sleek green head feathers and a slender crimson bill. The female has cinnamon head feathers with a ragged crest.

Mockingbird (Northern): An excellent mimic, the mockingbird repeats strings of songs from other birds. Their songs vary from region to region, depending on the other birds in their habitat!

Mourning dove: The soft cooing of a dove at dawn or dusk is often mistaken for the hooting of an owl. Its small head and plump body form a telltale silhouette.

Raven (common): This smart and playful bird is an aerial acrobat, sometimes turning somersaults or rolls in the air. Ravens are equally at home near people or in wilderness.

Red-tailed hawk: The red-tail soars above forests and fields, fanning its conspicuous rusty red tail. When perched, its brown back and streaked breast allow it to hide in plain sight.

Robin (American): Often considered a sign of spring, these orange-breasted members of the thrush family may stay around all year, feeding on fruit when worms and insects are scarce.

Starling (European): Introduced from Europe in the nineteenth century, the starling has spread throughout North America to become one of our most abundant songbirds.

Turkey vulture: Its bald pink head looks fearsome, but the vulture is a scavenger— an animal that only eats prey that has already been killed.

Wild turkey: It's not unusual to see flocks of these bold birds strutting across lawns, sidewalks, and streets even in urban areas.

To see photos of these birds, go to The Cornell Lab of Ornithology website at *www.allaboutbirds.org.*

Author's Note

I grew to love birds by watching them from my kitchen window in upstate New York. As a child, I read the *Birds of North America* Golden Guide cover to cover, and memorized pictures of birds with fantastic names like yellow-bellied sapsucker and magnificent frigate bird. Years later, when I finally saw them in real life I recognized them like old friends!

Different types of bird counts go on at various times around the world. Some focus on numbers of migrating birds or breeding birds, while others may count only particular species. The Christmas Bird Count (CBC) is an annual census of birds run by the National Audubon Society. It got its name because it occurs during the winter holidays. CBC volunteers perform counts in regional groups called "count circles." I joined a circle like the one in the story more than fifteen years ago, and I have only missed one year since.

Big Al is based on Al Sgroi, who has led our team for as long as I've been on it, and many years before that. He's an amazing birder, but he's not a trained scientist. That's what's so special about the CBC. Anyone interested in birds can join in. The more you observe birds, the better birder you become. When ordinary people work with professionals to do scientific research, it's known as citizen science. Started in 1900, the CBC is one of the longest running Citizen Science Surveys in the world!

Because the Christmas Bird Count includes the entire Western Hemisphere, a huge amount of information is collected. Bird scientists called ornithologists use count data to keep track of how birds are doing. Data can show when an endangered species, such as the bald eagle, is making a comeback, or when climate change causes a southern species, such as the Carolina wren, to expand its range northward. It also shows rises and falls in *resident* birds, those that live with us year round, and *migrants*, birds that travel south each winter in search of food. Most importantly, it unites people across many countries in helping to understand and protect these fascinating creatures.

If you think participating in a Christmas Bird Count sounds like fun, visit the National Audubon Society website at *www.audubon.org/conservation/science/christmas-bird-count* to find a count circle nearby.

Below are a few resources you can use to start your own bird count or simply to enjoy our beautiful birds.

"All About Birds." The Cornell Lab of Ornithology. Website at *www.allaboutbirds.org.*

"Audubon Guide to North American Birds." Website at *www.audubon.org.*

Peterson, Roger Tory. *Peterson First Guide to Birds of North America.* Boston: Houghton Mifflin, 1998.

Robbins, Chandler S., Bertel Bruun, and Herbert S. Zim, illustrated by Arthur Singer. *Birds of North America: A Guide to Field Identification.* New York: St. Martin's Press, 2001.

Sibley, David Allen. *The Sibley Guide to Bird Life and Behavior.* New York: Knopf, 2009.

Sill, Cathryn, illustrated by John Sill. *About Birds: A Guide for Children.* Atlanta, GA: Peachtree, 2013.